Penny
and the
Penguin

Kirin Daugharty

Using her animation skills and experience with the natural world, Kirin shows some of the secret lives of nature's most obvious creatures.

Published by CreateSpace.com
Copyright © 2012 by Kirin Daugharty.

ISBN-13: 978-1453895030
ISBN-10: 1453895035

Library of Congress Control Number: 2011963099
CreateSpace, North Charleston, SC

For information please visit www.kirind.blogspot.com.

Summary: Ever wonder how a penguin flies?

For Chris.

Penny walked along the shoreline, wandering away from her field trip, when something caught her eye.

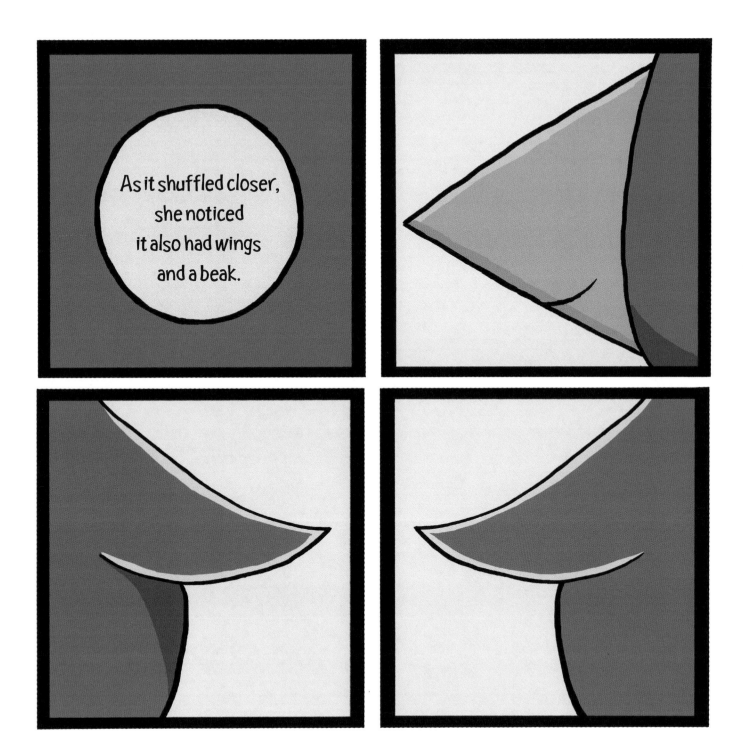

Watching the stubby bird struggle up the rocks, Penny wondered why penguins didn't fly like other birds. It sure would make life easier. "I bet," she thought, "that no one ever taught them how to fly."

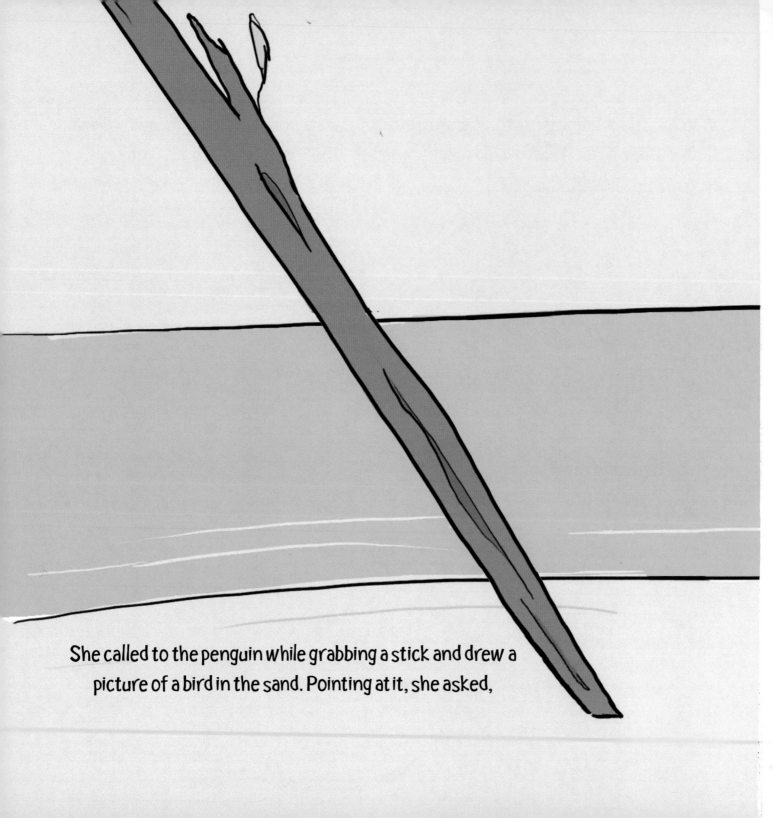

She called to the penguin while grabbing a stick and drew a picture of a bird in the sand. Pointing at it, she asked,

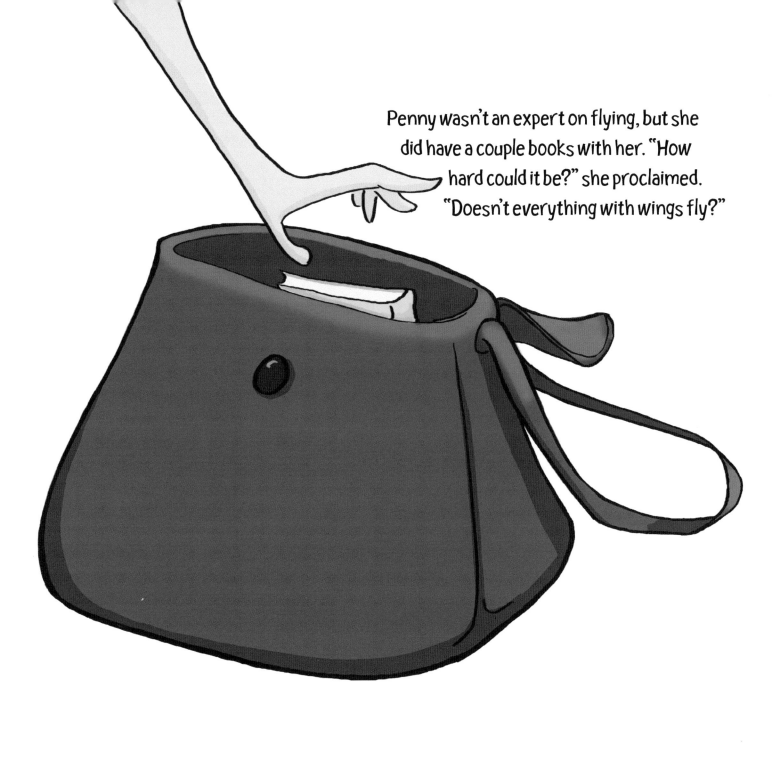

Penny wasn't an expert on flying, but she did have a couple books with her. "How hard could it be?" she proclaimed. "Doesn't everything with wings fly?"

Determined with her new mission, she opened her book for the penguin and pointed to a picture of an eagle soaring through the sky. But the penguin only wanted to eat the picture of the fish on the opposite page.

Penny thought for a bit. How else could she teach a penguin how to fly?

Across the path a set of swings rocking in the breeze gave Penny another idea.

She lay down across one of the swings and stretched out her arms. "Wee!" she said as she swung back and forth, flapping her arms like wings.

Meanwhile the penguin clumsily climbed up the ladder of a nearby slide and slipped down on his belly, landing with a POOF in the dirt below. Over and over again he slid.

This made the penguin quite dirty.

"I never thought it would be so hard to teach a penguin how to fly," sighed Penny.

"Aha!" She noticed the beach across the way. It was dotted with ducks. "I will show him how real birds fly."

As they approached the beach, the paddling of ducks took off into the bright blue sky. Penny pointed to the ducks as their wings pulled them higher into the air.

But instead of flying into the sky like the ducks, the penguin played and splashed in the water.

Penny kicked the dirt, feeling frustrated that she had failed to teach the penguin how to fly.

Her teacher called to her. Defeated, Penny climbed back up the cliff. She paused before rejoining her group. It was then that she looked back to see the penguin swimming through the ocean and noticed something amazing.

His wings flapped up and down just like the ducks. And he soared through the water like an eagle. A smile crept upon her face as she realized he was **flying!**

Penny gasped in wonder. He was so elegant. His graceful soaring was a far cry from his awkward struggle up the rocks.

She ran back to tell her group the exciting news.

"I taught a penguin how to fly!"

Under water of course.

THE END

Penguin Fun Facts!

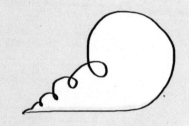

Did you know that there aren't any penguins at the North Pole? There are about seventeen species of penguin found throughout the southern hemisphere, and only a few of them live full-time in the Antarctic regions. Most live in warm climates, such as the Humboldt from South America, the fairy penguins from Australia and New Zealand, and the black-footed penguin from Africa. Galapagos penguins are the only ones who live north of the equator. But only slightly.

Penguins have the same strong flying muscles as a seagull, but an ostrich and a kiwi do not. Can you think of why that would be?

Penguins have short, broad, and closely spaced feathers to help keep water away from their skin so they can stay warm and dry.

About the Author

Kirin Daugharty received her Bachelor of Fine Arts degree in animation from the University of the Arts in Philadelphia.

She created characters for, and animated on, several television shows before migrating towards conservation and now works for the Greater Los Angeles Zoo Association. Kirin lives in the Los Angeles area with her husband and menagerie that includes some small carnivores and an invertebrate.

14443276R00020

Made in the USA
Charleston, SC
11 September 2012